Ms. Jo-Jo Is a Yo-Yo!

Dan Gutman

Pictures by Jim Paillot

HARPER

An Imprint of HarperCollinsPublishers

Thanks to Donna Deodato, and to my
Facebook and Twitter followers.

My Weirder-est School #7: Ms. Jo-Jo Is a Yo-Yo!
Text copyright © 2021 by Dan Guttman
Illustrations copyright © 2021 by Jim Paillot
For information address HarperCollins Children's Books, a division of
HarperCollins Publishers, 195 Broadway, New York, NY 10007.
www.harpercollinschildrens.com
ISBN 978-0-06-291040-0 (pbk bdg)   ISBN 978-0-06-291041-7 (lib. bdg)

Typography by Laura Mock
21 22 23 24 25 PC/BRR 10 9 8 7 6 5 4 3 2 1

First Edition

Contents

The FAR Test

My name is A.J. and I know what you're thinking. You're thinking I should watch my mouth.

"Watch your mouth, A.J.," my teacher Mr. Cooper is always telling me.

I don't get it. Grown-ups are always telling me to watch my mouth. How can

I watch my mouth? It's right under my eyes. I can't watch it.

I can't watch my ears, either, because they're over on the sides of my head. I tried to watch them, but they were too far away. I could watch my nose, but then I'd be cross-eyed.

So basically, I can't watch any of the stuff on my face, unless I look in a mirror.

The point is, I was at Ella Mentry School last week when the whole third grade got called down to the all-porpoise room. I don't know why they call it the all-porpoise room. There are no dolphins in there.

So we lined up and walked a million

hundred miles. When we finally got to the all-porpoise room, you'll never believe who was up on the stage.

It was Dr. Carbles, the president of the Board of Education!*

He's a mean man who drives a tank to school. What is his problem? Dr. Carbles was standing next to our principal, Mr. Klutz, who has no hair at all. He used to have hair, but it fell out a long time ago. Nobody knows why.

"Ten . . . hut!" shouted Dr. Carbles.

Why was he counting huts? There weren't any huts in the all-porpoise room.

---

*I should be on the Board of Education, because nobody's more bored of education than I am.

What do huts have to do with anything? But everybody stood at attention, as if we were soldiers.

"I have an announcement to make," Dr. Carbles shouted. "I called you in here to tell you blah blah blah blah one week from today all the students at Ella Mentry School will be taking a standardized test blah blah blah blah. You third graders will take the Fundamental Arithmetic/Reading Test."

FUNDAMENTAL
ARITHMETIC/
READING
TEST

Ugh, I hate standardized tests. A big groan spread across the all-porpoise room.

Dr. Carbles held up a sign that said "Fundamental Arithmetic/Reading Test." We all started elbowing each other and giggling because we realized that the first letters of the Fundamental Arithmetic/Reading Test spelled "FART."

Anytime anybody says anything that sounds like "fart," you have to giggle and elbow the person next to you. That's the first rule of being a kid.

"Quiet!" shouted Dr. Carbles. "Sit *down*!"

We sat down.

"Dr. Carbles said FART," I whispered to my friend Michael, who never ties his shoes.

"What do you think is going to be on the F.A.R.T.?" whispered Ryan, who will eat anything, even stuff that isn't food.

"I heard the F.A.R.T. is really hard," whispered Neil, who we call the nude kid even though he wears clothes.

"What happens if we fail the F.A.R.T.?" whispered Alexia, this girl who rides a skateboard all the time.

"I'm going to study for the F.A.R.T. as soon as I get home from school," whispered Andrea, this annoying girl with curly brown hair.

"Me too," whispered Emily, who does everything Andrea does.

Everybody in the all-porpoise room was buzzing about the F.A.R.T. But not like bees.

That would be weird. Mr. Klutz held up his hand and made a peace sign, which means shut up. But everybody ignored him.

"STOP SAYING FART!" shouted Dr. Carbles. "Watch your mouths!"

Even the teachers were freaking out about the F.A.R.T.

"Oh no, not the F.A.R.T.," groaned Mr. Cooper.

Mrs. Roopy, our librarian, slapped her

own forehead. Mr. Docker, our science teacher, rolled his eyes. Mrs. Jaffee, our vice principal, put her head in her hands. One of the other third-grade teachers slumped in her seat. The teachers must hate standardized tests just as much as kids do.

Everybody in the all-porpoise room was complaining about the F.A.R.T.

"Quiet!" shouted Dr. Carbles. "You kids had better score high on the Fundamental Arithmetic/Reading Test. Or else! Blah blah blah blah. Now get out of here! Go back to your classes! Beat it!"

"Okay, Pringle up, everybody," said Mr. Cooper.

We lined up like Pringles and marched out of the all-porpoise room.

"Left! Right! Left! Right!" shouted Dr. Carbles.

It took a million hundred hours to march back to our classroom. When we passed by the front office, I saw Dr. Carbles yelling at Mr. Klutz.

"At last, I'll be able to shut down this terrible school," Dr. Carbles said, rubbing his hands together. "You'll be finished, Klutz! Finished! For good! Bwa-ha-ha!"

Anytime grown-ups rub their hands together and say "bwa-ha-ha," you know they want to take over the world. That's the first rule of being a grown-up.

"But . . . but . . . but . . ." said Mr. Klutz.

I giggled because Mr. Klutz said "but," which sounds just like "butt" even though there's only one *t*.

"Do you think Dr. Carbles would *really* shut down our school?" asked Andrea.

"He can do anything he wants," said Alexia. "He's the president of the Board of Education. That's like being a king."

Wait a minute. That's when it hit me. If Dr. Carbles shuts down our school, we won't have to go to school anymore.

Sounds good to me!

What's the problem?

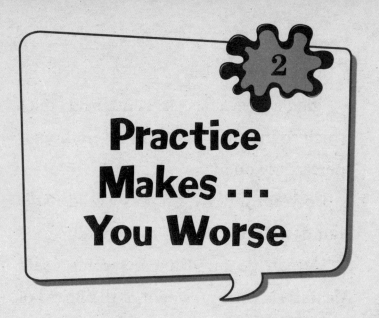

Practice Makes ... You Worse

The next day, Mr. Cooper came running into the class, all excited. Mr. Cooper thinks he's a superhero, and he wears a cape. What's up with that?

"We have five days to get ready for the F.A.R.T.," he announced. "We're not going to let Dr. Carbles shut down Ella Mentry School, are we, kids?"

"No!" shouted all the girls.

"Yes!" shouted all the boys.

"We're gonna fight for our school!" said Mr. Cooper. "Isn't that right, kids?"

"Yes!" shouted all the girls.

"No!" shouted all the boys.

There were some basic disagreements about education between the boys and the girls.

"You kids are going to *crush* the F.A.R.T.!" yelled Mr. Cooper.

"CRUSH . . . THE . . . F.A.R.T.!" Ryan chanted as he stood up. "CRUSH . . . THE . . . F.A.R.T.!"

We all jumped up and started chanting "CRUSH THE F.A.R.T.!"

Chanting is cool. You should chant stuff

13

whenever you can. That's the first rule of being a kid.

Mr. Cooper lowered his voice to a whisper, like he was going to tell us a big secret.

"I'm going to tell you a big secret," he whispered.

"Oooh, I love secrets!" said Alexia.

"I went on the internet," said Mr. Cooper, "and I downloaded a practice F.A.R.T. This will help to prepare you for the *real* F.A.R.T."

"I love practice tests!" said Andrea, who loves *any* kind of test, because it gives her the chance to show everybody how smart she is.

"Me too," said Emily, of course.

What is their problem? I hate *all* tests, real or practice.

Andrea waved her hand in the air like she was washing a big window with a sponge.

"Yes, Andrea?" asked Mr. Cooper.

"Is the F.A.R.T. a multiple-choice test?" she asked.

Ugh. I hate multiple-choice tests. A multiple-choice test is a test that has more than one choice for the answers, so it has the perfect name. They give you the right answer. It's staring you in the face. But they also throw in a bunch of *wrong* answers so you don't know which answer is the right one. That's *mean*! It would be a lot easier if multiple-choice tests only gave you one choice.*

"No, Andrea," said Mr. Cooper. "It's not multiple-choice. The F.A.R.T. is a fill-in-the-blanks test."

Oh, good! Filling in blanks is a lot easier. You can write anything you want.

Mr. Cooper told us to take out our number two pencils. We all started giggling because Mr. Cooper said "number two." Anytime a grown-up says "number two," you should giggle. Because we all

---

*It's like when you go to the supermarket for toothpaste. They have mint toothpaste, whitening toothpaste, toothpaste that fights plaque, toothpaste in different sizes. Too many choices! I just want toothpaste. And I don't even *like* brushing my teeth!

know what number two means, and it has nothing to do with pencils.

"I'm going to pass out—" Mr. Cooper said.

"He's going to pass out!" shouted Ryan.

"Call an ambulance!" shouted Michael.

"I'm going to pass out the practice tests," said Mr. Cooper.

"Oh," said Ryan and Michael.

"This will be just like a real F.A.R.T.," Mr. Cooper explained as he handed each of us a sheet of paper. "The reading questions are on the front, and the arithmetic questions are on the back. You'll have ten minutes to complete both sides. Ready? Set? Go!"

Mr. Cooper set a timer. I looked at the first paragraph on the sheet. It said: *One* day, Tony and Maria were walking home from school. They stopped off at a store that was selling bicycles . . . blah blah blah blah.

There was other stuff about Tony and Maria getting into trouble or something. I didn't read the whole thing. Then it asked: *What is the main idea of this paragraph?*

Well, *that* was easy. I filled in the blank by writing: Tony and Maria should take the bus.

Duh, right? I looked at the next question: *Jack and Jill went up the hill to fetch a pail of water. Jack fell down and broke his crown, and Jill came tumbling after. What is the lesson of this story?*

It was obvious! The lesson of the story is that Jack and Jill were dummies who should get water out of the faucet in their house, like normal people. I wrote that down.

"This is a piece of cake," whispered Ryan, who sits next to me.

Huh? What did cake have to do with anything? Ryan is weird.

I looked at the next question. It was a really long paragraph. I didn't read every word, but it had something to do with birds and bats. I scanned down to the bottom, where the question was: *How are bats different from birds?*

That was easy. I wrote this in the blank: You can't hit a ball with a bird.

I looked at the next question: *Look at this picture. What is going to happen next?*

I looked at the picture. It was a drawing

of a guy carrying an umbrella while two kids were tossing a ball back and forth and some lady was putting food on a picnic table.

What?! *Anything* could happen next. How was I supposed to know what was going to happen next? I raised my hand.

"How are we supposed to know what happens next?" I asked Mr. Cooper.

"Use your imagination," he replied.

Hmmm. I used my imagination and filled in the blank: Next, a bear will attack the family and eat them. So instead of the family having a nice picnic, the bear has one.

I answered a few more questions like that. The F.A.R.T. was *easy*! I was halfway done, and I was crushing it. I gave Ryan a

thumbs-up.

I turned over the sheet to work on the math questions. Ugh. I hate math.

The first question had a picture of a shoebox with a bunch of spiders in it. The question was: *Is the number of objects in the box odd or even?*

Clearly, the answer was: Odd, because it would be odd to put spiders in a shoebox. Who *does* that? I wrote that down and looked at the next question: *A pen costs $7. How many pens could you buy for $35?*

Why would I want to buy pens? I can just borrow a pen from Ryan. He has lots of pens. Duh! I wrote that down and moved on to the next question: *Your favorite TV show is 30 minutes long. How many episodes can you watch in 2 hours?*

Hmmm. That depends on how many TVs you watch at the same time. I wrote down the number 10 and moved on to the next question: *Sammy has 32 socks, which he puts into pairs. How many pairs of socks can he make?*

How should I know? My mom does the laundry. I wrote: O.

I looked at the next question: *Tommy lost 2 teeth. The tooth fairy left 4 dimes, 3 nickels, and 2 quarters under his pillow. How much money did the tooth fairy leave for Tommy?*

Ha, it was a trick question! Everybody knows the tooth fairy doesn't exist. And if she *did* exist, she wouldn't be so cheap. I wrote that down and went on to the next question: *A paper clip is made from 6 inches of wire. How much wire would you need to make 5 paper clips?*

What?! Who makes their own paper

clips? Can't you just buy them at the store? I wrote that down and looked at the next question: *A new skateboard costs $47.99. Joe has $12.54. How much more money does he need to buy a new skateboard?*

I know a lot about skateboards. The obvious answer was: No money. I wrote that Joe should wait until his birthday or Christmas so he can get the skateboard for free.

I looked at the next question: *You have 8 plums in a basket. You give some of them away, leaving 2 plums in the basket. How many plums did you give away?*

Me, I'd give away *all* the plums. I hate

plums. I wrote that down and looked at the next question: *Maggie went trick-or-treating and collected 100 candy bars. Her mom took 79 of them away to save for later. How many candy bars did Maggie eat on Halloween night?*

A hundred, of course. Maggie found where her mom hid the candy bars and ate them all. I wrote that down.

That was the last question on the page. Time hadn't even run out yet. That's how easy the test was.

A minute later, Mr. Cooper's alarm buzzed.

"Pencils down!" he said, and he collected the papers.

"How long will it take to grade the test?" asked Andrea.

"A few minutes," Mr. Cooper replied.

He sat at his desk to grade the tests. And you'll never believe who poked his head into the door at that moment.

Nobody! Why would you poke your head into a door? That would hurt. But you'll never believe who poked his head into the door*way*.

It was Mr. Klutz.

"So how did you kids do on your practice test?" he asked us.

"We *crushed* it!" I told him.

It took a million hundred minutes for Mr. Cooper to finish checking our answers. Finally, he looked up. We were all on the edge of our seats.

Well, not really. We were sitting in the middle of our seats. But there was electricity in the air.

Well, not really. If there was electricity in the air, we all would have been electrocuted. But it was really tense!

"So, how did the kids make out?" asked Mr. Klutz.

Ugh! Gross! We weren't making out!

Mr. Cooper didn't look very happy. "They all failed the test," he said sadly.

WHAT?!

"Even *me*?" asked Andrea, who never fails anything.

"The whole class failed," said Mr. Cooper.

Everybody started yelling and screaming and hooting and hollering and freaking out.

"What are we going to do?" shouted Emily. She looked like she was going to cry, like always.

"I can't believe it!" shouted Michael.

"They're going to shut down the school!" shouted Neil.

"I'm going to lose my job!" shouted Mr. Cooper.

"Me too!" shouted Mr. Klutz.

"My life is ruined!" shouted Alexia.

"This is going to look bad on my record," shouted Andrea. "I won't get into Harvard!"

I looked out in the hallway. And you'll

never believe who was standing out there watching all this.

It was Dr. Carbles. He had a big smile on his face, and he was rubbing his hands together.

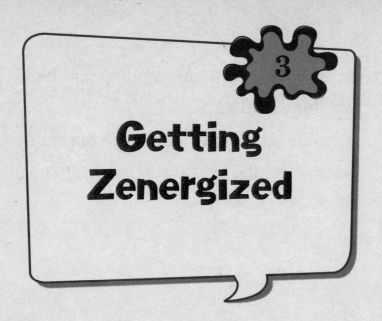

Getting Zenergized

There were four days until the F.A.R.T., and everybody was stressed about it. That's when Mr. Klutz came to visit our class again. He was with our school counselor, Dr. Brad, who has crazy hair and looks like a mad scientist in a horror movie.

"Dr. Carbles wants to make you nervous

so you'll fail the F.A.R.T.," said Mr. Klutz. "So I thought Dr. Brad might be able to help."

"Zee whole school ees feeling zo much stress," said Dr. Brad, who talks funny. "Vee all need to calm down about zis test."

"Dr. Brad thinks he can help us relax," said Mr. Klutz.

"Yes, I vant to try somezing," said Dr. Brad. "Zeet down, Meester Klutz."

Mr. Klutz sat in a chair. Dr. Brad took a shiny metal watch out of his pocket. It was attached to a chain. He dangled the watch in front of Mr. Klutz's face and began slowly swinging it back and forth.

"Look at zis veddy closely," Dr. Brad said

softly. "Eet vill help you to be calm."

"Are you hypnotizing me?" Mr. Klutz asked as he stared at the watch.

"Yes," said Dr. Brad. "See zuh shiny vatch? Stare at eet as eet svings back and forth. Zee eyelids feel a leetle heavy, yes?"

"Heavy . . ." Mr. Klutz mumbled.

I know all about hypnosis. People will do *anything* when they're hypnotized. One time, I hypnotized Andrea. She climbed up to the roof of the school and screamed at the police when they tried to get her to come down. That was the greatest day of my life.*

"Stare at zuh vatch as eet svings," said Dr. Brad, "back and forth . . . back and forth . . . back and forth . . ."

"Back and forth . . ." repeated Mr. Klutz, like a robot.

"Feeling zleepy?" asked Dr. Brad.

"Sleepy . . ." moaned Mr. Klutz.

"Zoon you vill be in a deep zleep," said Dr. Brad. "You vill be relaxed. You vill be calm. You vill stop stressing about zee test."

"Relaxed . . . calm," moaned Mr. Klutz.

---

* You can read all about it in a book called *Dr. Brad Has Gone Mad!*

"It's working!" shouted Ryan. "He hypnotized Mr. Klutz!"

That's when the weirdest thing in the history of the world happened. Mr. Klutz suddenly stood up, flapped his arms, and started to cluck like a chicken.

"Bok bok bok," said Mr. Klutz.

"Vut are you doink?" asked Dr. Brad.

"I'm a chicken!" shouted Mr. Klutz, running around the class and flapping his arms. "Bok bok bok. Where can I lay my eggs?"

"Mr. Klutz is nuts!" Michael shouted.

Mr. Klutz ran a few laps around the classroom, looking for a place to lay his eggs. Then, just as suddenly, he stopped acting like a chicken. He looked like himself again.

"I wasn't in a trance," he told us. "I wasn't hypnotized for a second. I was just kidding."

"Eet only verks on zum people," said Dr. Brad.

"Exactly," said Mr. Klutz. "Even if it had worked, it would be impossible to hypnotize the whole *school*. But I have another idea that might help lower everybody's stress level."

He went out in the hall for a minute. When he came back, a lady was with him. She had long black hair, and she wasn't wearing shoes.

"This is Ms. Jo-Jo," Mr. Klutz announced. "She's a wellness expert."

"She digs wells?" I asked.

"No, dumbhead!" said Andrea. "She makes people *feel* well."

"I knew that," I lied. I was going to say something mean to Andrea, but I couldn't come up with anything good.

"Namaste," said Ms. Jo-Jo. She bowed to us with her hands pressed together.

"HUH?" we all said, which is also "HUH" backward.

"Nah-mah-stay," said Ms. Jo-Jo slowly. "That means 'the light in me bows to the light in you.' "

"Why don't you have shoes on?" asked Michael.

"Shoes are jail cells for the feet," Ms. Jo-Jo replied.

That's weird.

Ms. Jo-Jo had a machine with her. It looked sort of like a big toaster. She plugged it into the wall socket.

"What does that thing do?" asked Ryan.

"This is a Mood Meter," she replied. "It reads the stress level of people in a room."

Ms. Jo-Jo turned on the Mood Meter, and a few seconds later it beeped.

"Ooooh," she said. "The stress level in this room is over a hundred. That's *very* high. You kids must be *really* stressed out."

"Yes," said Mr. Klutz. "Everyone is on edge because they have to take the Fundamental Arithmetic/Reading Test in a few days."

"If our school doesn't do well," added

Mr. Cooper, "the president of the Board of Education is going to shut it down. Can you help us?"

"I'll try," said Ms. Jo-Jo. "I've never worked with children before. But I'll do my best. Let's do a little exercise. Everybody close your shoes and take off your eyes."

"HUH?" we all asked.

"I mean, take off your shoes and close your eyes," said Ms. Jo-Jo.

Oh, that's different.

We took off our shoes and closed our eyes.

"Now take a deep breath," said Ms. Jo-Jo.

We all took deep breaths, even the grown-ups.

"Hold it . . . and let it out," she said softly.

"In . . . and out. In . . . and out."

"I already know how to breathe," I said. "If I didn't know how to breathe, I'd be dead."

Nobody laughed at my joke. They were all breathing in and out.

"Now picture a beam of energy," said Ms. Jo-Jo. "Ride it out of your body, up into the air, and toward the stars."

I pretended that I was riding a beam of energy out of my body and into outer space. It was cool.

"Very good," said Ms. Jo-Jo. "Now repeat after me—"

"After me," we all repeated.

"No," said Ms. Jo-Jo. "I mean *repeat* after me."

"After me . . . after me . . . after me," we all repeated. "After me . . . after me . . . after me . . . after me . . . after me . . . after me . . . after me . . . after me . . . after me . . . after me . . . after me . . . after me . . . after me . . .

after me . . . after me . . ."

We repeated "after me" for like a million hundred minutes. Finally, Ms. Jo-Jo said we could stop repeating "after me" and open our eyes.

"How do you feel?" asked Ms. Jo-Jo.

"I feel more relaxed already," said Mr. Klutz.

"Me too!" said Ryan.

"Me three," said Neil.

"Me four," said Alexia.

In case you were wondering, everybody said they felt more relaxed. Ms. Jo-Jo went over to look at the Mood Meter.

"Look!" she said. "Your stress level is down to ninety-four. That's still very high, but it's a big improvement. If we can get your stress level down to fifty, you will be *really* relaxed."

"Fantastic!" exclaimed Mr. Klutz. "What do you call that breathing exercise?"

Ms. Jo-Jo replied, "I call it zenergizing."

Toga Party!

Ms. Jo-Jo's zenergizing was so successful that Mr. Klutz hired her to come back and help us every day leading up to the big F.A.R.T. It was in three days.

"Namaste," Ms. Jo-Jo said as she came into the class and bowed to us.

"Namaste," we all replied.

"What are we going to do today, Ms. Jo-Jo?" asked Neil.

"Are we going to get zenergized again?" asked Alexia.

"No, today we're going to do yoga," replied Ms. Jo-Jo.

I never did yoga before, so I decided that it's dumb. Anything you never did before is dumb. That's the first rule of being a kid.

"Ooooh, I *love* yoga!" shouted Andrea, who loves everything grown-ups love. "I signed up to take a yoga class after school."

Andrea takes classes in *everything* after school. If they gave classes in blowing your nose, she would take that class so she could get better at it.

"I love yoga *too*!" shouted Emily, who loves everything Andrea loves.

"My mom takes a class in goat yoga," said Ryan. "They do yoga exercises while goats climb all over them."

Everybody laughed, because we were picturing people doing yoga while goats were climbing all over them.

"That's ridiculous!" said Ms. Jo-Jo. "I would never do anything that silly."

"So what kind of yoga are *we* going to do?" Andrea asked.

"Turtle yoga," replied Ms. Jo-Jo. "I call it . . . Toga."

She went out in the hall and came back

wheeling a bunch of yoga mats and a big aquarium filled with turtles.

"Where do you think Ms. Jo-Jo got all those turtles?" Ryan whispered to me.

"From Rent-a-Turtle," I whispered back. "You can rent *anything*."

"These are my emotional-support turtles," said Ms. Jo-Jo. "They help me relax."

"They're adorable!" said Emily, who thinks all animals are adorable.

"Lie down on these shoes and take off your yoga mats," said Ms. Jo-Jo. "I mean, take off your shoes and lie down on these yoga mats."

Ms. Jo-Jo got on the floor and showed us something called the cow pose. It's a pose that makes you look like a cow, so it has the perfect name. While we all did the cow pose, she put a turtle on each of our backs. It was weird feeling, but cool too.

"Turn off your eyes and close your brain," said Ms. Jo-Jo. "I mean, turn off your brain and close your eyes. Are you feeling your inner turtle?"

"I am!" said Andrea.

"Turtles are ticklish!" said Alexia.

"My turtle is walking on my back!" said Michael.

"Turtle yoga is fun!" said Ryan.

"Imagine that you're playing fetch with your turtle," said Ms. Jo-Jo.

It's really hard to play fetch with a turtle.

You throw a stick or something and the turtle doesn't come back with it for, like, an hour.

Doing yoga with turtles was ridorkulous, but fun. Ms. Jo-Jo taught us a bunch of poses: downward-facing dog, lion pose, cobra pose, tree pose. In the middle of it, Mr. Klutz came in.

"I just wanted to see how the kids were making out," he said.

Ugh, gross!

"We're having a toga party!" Ryan told him.

"TO-GA! TO-GA! TO-GA!" I chanted.

I thought that everybody was going to chant with me. But nobody did. Everybody was just looking at me. I hate when that happens.

Suddenly, for no reason, Emily started freaking out.

"What's the matter, Emily?" asked Andrea.

"I think my turtle just peed on me!" Emily shouted.

It was hilarious. Everybody was laughing, even Emily. We were all relaxed and having fun.

Ms. Jo-Jo went over to check the Mood Meter.

"The turtle yoga must be working," she said. "See? Your stress level has dropped down to seventy-six!"

"Great job, Ms. Jo-Jo!" said Mr. Klutz.

"Namaste," she replied.*

---

* This book comes with a money-back guarantee. If you're not completely satisfied, we guarantee that you won't get your money back.

Sense and Non-Sense

There were only two more days until the F.A.R.T. We were still nervous about the test, but thanks to Ms. Jo-Jo, everybody was getting relaxed. We couldn't wait to see what she was going to do with us next.

"Namaste," she said as she walked into our classroom. She was carrying a tray with a bunch of paper cups on it.

"Namaste," we all replied.

"Are you kids getting relaxed?" she asked.

"Yeah!" we all said.

"Great! Get on your shoes and take off the floor."

HUH?

"I mean get on the floor and take off your shoes."

Oh, that's different.

"Today we're going to relax your senses," said Ms. Jo-Jo as she gave each of us a cup with some green stuff in it. "First, your sense of taste. Drink this."

"What is it, mint?" I asked as I took a sip.

"It's celery juice," she replied. "It's a superfood."

Ugh! Celery juice tasted like celery, but even yuckier. I thought I was gonna die. Everybody hated the taste, except for Andrea and Emily, of course. They asked for seconds.

Ms. Jo-Jo felt bad that we didn't like her celery juice, so she gave each of us a pacifier, which are those things they give to crying babies to keep them quiet.

"What am I supposed to do with *this*?" I asked.

"Suck on it, of course," said Ms. Jo-Jo.

"But they're for babies!" complained Ryan.

"Aren't we all just babies that got bigger?" asked Ms. Jo-Jo. "Pacifiers relax children of *all* ages."

I sucked on the pacifier. She was right. It *was* relaxing.

Next, Ms. Jo-Jo went out in the hall and came back carrying a big tent, the kind you use when you go camping. She pushed some of our desks aside and opened up the tent in the middle of the classroom.

"What are we going to do with a tent?" asked Michael.

"It's not just a tent," Ms. Jo-Jo replied as she climbed inside. "It's an Aroma Dome. It will help relax your sense of smell. Come on in!"

We all climbed into the Aroma Dome. Ms. Jo-Jo lit some stinky candles and told us to breathe in the essential oils. Then she took a banana out of her pocket.

"What's that for?" Neil asked.

Ms. Jo-Jo peeled the banana and told Neil to rub the peel on his ears. He did. This was getting weird.

"Banana oil calms your nerves and

relieves your stress," she told Neil as she ate the banana. "Go ahead, everybody try it."

I wasn't going to rub a banana peel on my ears. No way! That was just *too* weird.

But everybody else in the class started rubbing the banana peel on their ears. I didn't want to look like the weird kid, so I rubbed the banana peel on my ears. It felt strange, but kind of nice.

"Your skin absorbs the vitamins from the banana," said Ms. Jo-Jo.

After that, she burned some green leafy stuff called sage. She said it promotes healing and gets rid of bad vibes, negative energy, and evil spirits. It also stinks. I was afraid it might set off the fire alarm.

"Ummm," said Andrea. "It smells nice in here."

"The Aroma Dome is like a rain forest," said Ms. Jo-Jo, "but without the forest.*

_____

* Or the rain.

Next, let's relax your sense of hearing."

She told us to get on the floor of the Aroma Dome and lie facedown. Then she took a bunch of big bowls out of a sack and put one bowl on each of our backs. This was getting *really* weird.

"What's with the bowls?" asked Alexia.

"This is called singing bowl therapy," said Ms. Jo-Jo. "Ready for a sound bath?"

She hit each bowl with her hand.

Boiiiiiinnnnngggg . . .

My bowl vibrated like crazy. It felt buzzy all over.

"Vibrational healing dates back to ancient times," said Ms. Jo-Jo. "It blocks out noise pollution and helps you escape from the stress of modern life. Isn't it soothing?"

Boiiiiiiinnnnngggg . . .

Boiiiiiiinnnnngggg . . .

"Invite calm into your brain," said Ms. Jo-Jo. "Unwind and go with the flow. Let the flow flow through your body."

Singing bowl therapy is cool. Ms. Jo-Jo let us switch bowls so we could feel different vibrations.

Boiiiiiiinnnnngggg . . .

Boiiiiiiinnnnngggg . . .

"Finally, we need to relax your sense of touch," Ms. Jo-Jo said as she collected up the bowls. "Everyone turn and face the student on your left."

I turned to my left.

It was Andrea. Uh-oh.

"This will *really* help you relax," said Ms. Jo-Jo. "I'd like you to gently massage that student's feet."

Noooooooo!

"I'm not going to touch your feet," I told Andrea.

"Arlo, you *have* to," Andrea replied. "Ms. Jo-Jo said so."

This was the worst moment of my life. I wanted to run away to Antarctica and go live with the penguins. Penguins didn't have to give each other foot massages.

I didn't want the guys to make fun of me for rubbing Andrea's feet. But Ryan was rubbing Neil's feet. Emily was rubbing

Michael's feet. Everybody was rubbing somebody else's feet. So I rubbed Andrea's feet.

Ugh. Disgusting! I thought I was gonna die.

"Oooooh!" Ryan said. "A.J. is rubbing Andrea's feet! They must be in LOVE!"

"When are you gonna get married?" asked Michael.

If those guys weren't my best friends, I

would hate them.

Ms. Jo-Jo had us do foot massages for a million hundred minutes.

"Okay, now all your senses should be relaxed," she said.

Ms. Jo-Jo climbed out of the Aroma Dome to check the Mood Meter. It said our stress level was down to sixty-two.

"WOW," we all said, which is "MOM" upside down. We were getting *really* relaxed!

Total Relaxation

It was our last day before the F.A.R.T. While we were putting our backpacks into our cubbies, I told Ryan that Ms. Jo-Jo must be *super* relaxed all the time. She probably *never* gets stressed out.

"She's cool as a cucumber," said Ryan.

HUH? What did cucumbers have to do with anything?

"Namaste," Ms. Jo-Jo said as she came into the class.

"Namaste," we replied.

Ms. Jo-Jo was carrying a bowl in her arms. I thought we might be doing more singing bowl therapy, but there were pink blocks in the bowl and an electrical cord hanging out of the bottom.

"What's *that*?" asked Emily.

"It's a crystal salt lamp," Ms. Jo-Jo replied.

She told us the crystal salt chunks were millions of years old and they came from Pakistan. She plugged the cord into the electrical outlet on the wall. The bowl gave off a warm, pink glow.

"I am grooving on it," said Ryan, nodding his head.

"Yeah, man," said Michael.

"The crystal salt lamp produces ions that change the electrical charge of the air," Ms. Jo-Jo explained. "This will boost your mood and balance your aura."

I had no idea what she was talking about.

"Now I have a special surprise," she told us. She went out in the hallway and came back with this thing that looked like a pyramid.

"What's *that*?" we all asked.

"In ancient Egypt," said Ms. Jo-Jo, "they believed that pyramids had a mysterious secret energy. They line up with the earth's magnetic field."

The pyramid was actually a bunch of pyramids that fit inside each other, like a stack of ice cream cones. Ms. Jo-Jo gave each of us a pyramid.

"What are we supposed to do with it?" Andrea asked.

"You put it on your head, of course," replied Ms. Jo-Jo.

We put the pyramids on our heads.

"Good," said Ms. Jo-Jo. "Now repeat after me."

"After me . . . After me . . . After me . . ."
we repeated.

"The mind is infinite," she said.

"After me . . . After me . . . After me . . ."

"Turn off your mind, relax, and float downstream," she said.

"After me . . . After me . . . After me . . ."

"Love is love."*

"After me . . . After me . . . After me . . ."

"Feel your cosmic energy."

"After me . . . After me . . . After me . . ."

"Now, slowly bring yourself back to your awareness."

"After me . . . After me . . . After me . . ."

"Did you feel your heart rate slow

---

*Ugh, she said the L word!

down?" asked Ms. Jo-Jo.

"My heart slowed down so much that it almost stopped beating," said Neil.

"Good," said Ms. Jo-Jo. "Now I'm going to blow the ceremonial conch trumpet to help you return to reality."

She started blowing some weird trumpet thing. And you'll never believe who walked into the door at that moment.

Nobody! Walking into a door would hurt. I thought we went over that in chapter two. But you'll never believe who walked into the door*way*. It was Dr. Brad and Mr. Klutz!

We took the pyramids off our heads.

"Why were you wearing pyramids on your heads?" asked Mr. Klutz.

"Ms. Jo-Jo told us that pyramids create a mysterious secret energy force that lines up with the earth's magnetic field," Ryan explained.

I thought Mr. Klutz might be mad that we were wearing pyramids on our heads. But he wasn't.

"Hey, if wearing a pyramid on your head lowers your stress level, I'm all for it," he said.

Ms. Jo-Jo went over and checked the Mood Meter. It said our stress level was down to fifty! Everybody started cheering.

"The students are totally relaxed now, stress-free, and ready for your big F.A.R.T. tomorrow," said Ms. Jo-Jo.

"That is fantastic!" said Mr. Klutz. "We owe it all to you, Ms. Jo-Jo. I don't know how you did it."

"Vutever she did verks even better zan hypnosis!" said Dr. Brad.

Ms. Jo-Jo must be a genius. She should get the Nobel Prize. That's a prize they give out to people who don't have bells.

"Thank you," Ms. Jo-Jo replied. "I'm sure the students are going to crush the F.A.R.T. tomorrow."

"CRUSH THE F.A.R.T.!" I chanted as I jumped up. "CRUSH THE F.A.R.T.!"

I thought everybody was going to jump up and chant with me. But nobody jumped up. Nobody chanted. Everybody was looking at me.

I hate when that happens.

The Big FART

Finally, it was F.A.R.T. day, and I wasn't stressed at all. By this point, we were all so relaxed, *nothing* could stress us out.

"Namaste," Ms. Jo-Jo said when she came into our class. For the first time, she wasn't barefoot.

"Ms. Jo-Jo!" Alexia said. "You're wearing sandals!"

"Yes, this is a special occasion," she told us. "Do you like them? They're made from recycled Himalayan dream catchers."

"They're pretty!" said Andrea, who thinks everything girls wear is pretty.

"Good luck on the F.A.R.T. today," said Ms. Jo-Jo. "I'm sure you kids are going to do great!"

"We go with the flow, man," said Ryan.

"It is what it is," said Alexia.

"I'm so chill," said Neil, "I might fall asleep in the middle of the F.A.R.T."

"Whatever," I said.

That's when Dr. Carbles came in with Mr. Klutz. Dr. Carbles was rubbing his hands together.

"These kids are going to fail big-time," he said excitedly, "and Ella Mentry School will be shut down forever!"

"Oh, I think our students may surprise you," said Mr. Klutz. "They're totally relaxed and ready, thanks to Ms. Jo-Jo."

We took out our number two pencils and Dr. Carbles handed out the test sheets. The F.A.R.T. looked a lot like the practice test we had taken. The reading part was on one side and arithmetic was on the other side. We had ten minutes to finish both sides of the test.

"On your mark . . . Get set . . . Go!" said Dr. Carbles.

I looked at the first question. It was a story about a girl who doesn't know how to swim, so she takes swimming lessons. Then she's in a canoe that tips over and she saves her best friend's life. The question was: *What is the lesson of the story?*

It was obvious. I wrote: Instead of going

canoeing, she should take a turtle yoga class.

I looked at the next question. It was a long paragraph about two kids who find a secret cave with a magic lamp and a genie in it. The kids argue over the three wishes they should wish for. The question was: *What is the main idea of the paragraph?*

Well, *that* was easy. I wrote: Who cares? Those kids should turn off their minds, relax, and float downstream.

I looked at the next question. It was about a bunch of animals. The question was: *How are frogs different from toads? How are alligators different from crocodiles?*

I wrote: Instead of talking about the differences between living creatures, we should talk about the ways we're all the same.

I moved on to the next question: *Look at this picture. What is going to happen next?*

I looked at the picture. It showed a family of bunnies frolicking in a field, with a hunter stalking them in the corner.

I wrote: The bunnies are going to give each other foot massages and take a sound bath so they can feel their cosmic energy.

I answered a few more questions like that. Then I turned over the sheet to work

on the math questions. The first one was: *A pair of new shoes costs $50. How many pairs of shoes can Mary buy for $300?*

Simple! I wrote: None. Shoes are jail cells for the feet. I moved on to the next question: *It takes 25 minutes to play your favorite video game. How many games can you play in 2 hours?*

Easy! I wrote: None. Instead of playing video games, from now on I'm going to spend my free time sitting under the pyramid while sucking on a pacifier.

I moved on to the next question: *Josh lost his favorite action figure while playing with it on the school bus. A new one will cost $16. He has saved $5.60. How much more money does he need to replace his toy?*

I wrote: He should save up for a crystal salt lamp instead.

I looked at the next question: *There are five 12-inch pillows on a 96-inch couch. How much space should you put between each pillow so they are equally spaced on the couch?*

I wrote: Does it really matter? I mean, really? Climate change may make the earth uninhabitable. Why worry about where the pillows are placed on the couch?

I looked at the next question: *Johnny has 17 bananas. He gives some of them away, leaving him with 8 bananas. How many bananas did he give away?*

I wrote: I don't know, but Johnny should rub the

banana peels on his ears and drink some celery juice.

I looked at the next question: *Jane went trick-or-treating and collected 76 Kit Kat bars. Her parents took 52 of them away to save for later. How many Kit Kat bars did Jane eat that night?*

I wrote: None. Jane cut out sugar and became a vegan. Namaste. The light in me bows to the light in you.

That was the last question on the page.

Beeeeeep!

"Pencils down!" shouted Dr. Carbles.

We passed our papers up to Mr. Cooper so he could grade them. It took like a million hundred minutes. Mr. Klutz was hovering over his shoulder the whole time.

"How did the kids make out?" he asked.

Ugh, gross! We didn't make out!

"I just need one more minute," said Mr. Cooper.

While Mr. Cooper graded our tests,

there was *no* electricity in the air. *Nobody* was on pins and needles. We were all sitting in the middle of our seats. That's how relaxed we were.

Finally, Mr. Cooper put down his pencil and looked up.

"It's the moment of truth," said Dr. Carbles, rubbing his hands together.

Mr. Cooper said, "The result of the F.A.R.T. is . . ."*

---

*Don't look at the next page! Don't look at the next page! Don't look at the next page! Oh, you looked at the next page!

The Truth about Ms. Jo-Jo

"Everybody failed," said Mr. Cooper.

"WHAT?!" shouted Ms. Jo-Jo. "The whole class failed the test? How can that be? There must be some mistake!"

For the first time ever, she looked *really* upset.

"I'm sorry," said Mr. Cooper. "They failed."

To tell you the truth, I didn't care that we all failed the F.A.R.T. None of us cared. We were all so relaxed, nothing seemed to matter.

"Oh, well," I said. "It is what it is."

"Such is life," said Neil.

"Ya can't win 'em all," said Ryan.

"So it goes," said Michael.

"Life is too short to worry about silly tests anyway," said Mr. Klutz.

"There's no use crying over spilled milk," said Andrea.

HUH? What did milk have to do with anything?

The only person who seemed to care that we failed the F.A.R.T. was Dr. Carbles. He had a big grin on his face, and he was rubbing his hands together.

"That's it!" he shouted. "*Finally*, I have a reason to shut down Ella Mentry School! All the teachers are fired! Klutz, you're fired! At last my dreams have come true! Bwa-ha-ha!"*

There was total silence. You could have

---

* Be sure to rub your hands together and say "bwa-ha-ha" in your best evil, mad scientist voice.

heard a pin drop. But not a bowling pin. They make a lot of noise.

"Uh, does this mean we don't have to go to school anymore?" I asked.

"No!" shouted Dr. Carbles. "It means you little monsters will have to go to some *other* school! You'll probably be in third grade for the rest of your lives! Bwa-ha-ha!"

What?! Bummer in the summer! I thought that if our school closed down, we wouldn't have to go to school anymore.

This was the worst thing to happen since TV Turnoff Week! I wanted to run away to Antarctica and go live with the penguins. Penguins don't have to take the F.A.R.T.

"What about *me*?" asked Ms. Jo-Jo. She looked like she was about to cry.

"You're fired too!" shouted Dr. Carbles. "Beat it! And take your stinky candles with you!"

That's when Ms. Jo-Jo went nuts.

"Noooooo!" she shrieked. "How could the kids have failed? I worked so hard to get them relaxed."

"Maybe they were *too* relaxed," said Mr. Klutz.

"What am I going to do *now*?" shouted Ms. Jo-Jo. "I *need* this job! It's not fair! You told me to lower the kids' stress level, and that's exactly what I did! I can't take it!"

Ms. Jo-Jo was crying and shouting "I can't take it!" over and over again. Then she got down on the ground and started kicking her feet and beating her fists against the floor.

"You need to calm down, Ms. Jo-Jo!" said Mr. Klutz.

We all gathered around her on the floor.

"Take a deep breath, Ms. Jo-Jo," I told her. "Unwind and go with the flow."

"Breathe in . . . and out," said Andrea.

"Leave me alone!" Ms. Jo-Jo shouted. "I know how to breathe!"

Ms. Jo-Jo is a yo-yo! She was yelling and screaming and hooting and hollering and having a total temper tantrum.

I looked at the Mood Meter. It said the stress level was over a hundred.

That's when the weirdest thing in the history of the world happened. But I'm not going to tell you what it was.

Okay, okay, I'll tell you. But you have to read the next chapter. So nah-nah-nah boo-boo on you!

The Big Surprise Ending

Our teachers were going to be fired. The school was going to be shut down. Ms. Jo-Jo was having a major meltdown, kicking and screaming on the floor like a baby. I was going to be in third grade for the rest of my life. It was the worst day in the history of the world. My life was over.

Nobody knew what to say. Nobody knew what to do. Somebody had to think fast.

That's when Dr. Brad came running into the room. He took his watch out of his pocket, dangled it in front of Dr. Carbles's face, and began swinging it back and forth.

"Look at zis," he said softly.

"What are you doing?" Dr. Carbles asked, staring at the watch.

"Eezn't zis shiny?" asked Dr. Brad.

"Shiny . . ." mumbled Dr. Carbles.

"Stare at zuh shiny vatch as eet svings back and forth . . . back and forth . . . back and forth," said Dr. Brad.

"Back . . . and forth . . ." mumbled Dr. Carbles.

"Your eyelids are feeling a leetle heavy, no?" said Dr. Brad.

"Heavy . . ." Dr. Carbles mumbled, like a robot.

"Are you feeling zleepy?" asked Dr. Brad.

"Sleepy . . ."

"Zoon you vill be in a trance."

"Trance . . ."

It was working! Dr. Carbles was totally hypnotized!* We saw it with our own eyes!

Well, it would be pretty hard to see it with somebody *else's* eyes.

"You vill do everyzing I say," said Dr. Brad.

---

* Betcha didn't see THAT coming!

"Everything you say . . ." mumbled Dr. Carbles.

"And ven I snap my fingers, you vill vake up and not remember anyzing."

"Not remember anything . . ."

"Dr. Carbles, you vill keep Ella Mentry School open," said Dr. Brad.

"Keep school open . . ."

"None of zuh teachers vill be fired."

"No firing . . ."

That's when I got the greatest idea in the history of the world. I did something that I probably shouldn't have done. But I couldn't help it.

I ran over and shouted at Dr. Carbles, "You think you're a chicken!"

"Arlo, stop!" said Andrea. "That's not nice!"

"I'm a chicken . . ." mumbled Dr. Carbles.

"You need a place to lay your eggs," I

shouted at him.

"Lay eggs . . ." mumbled Dr. Carbles. "Bok bok bok!"

Dr. Carbles made more chicken sounds. Then he started running around the room, flapping his arms.

"I'm a chicken!" he shouted. "Where can I lay my eggs? Bok bok bok! I need a place to lay my eggs! Bok bok bok!"

Well, that's pretty much what happened. When Dr. Brad snapped his fingers, Dr. Carbles woke up and didn't remember anything. He had forgotten all about closing the school or firing the teachers. It was cool. You should have *been* there!

The only bad thing is that we'll have to keep going to Ella Mentry School. But at least I won't be in third grade for the rest of my life. Maybe Ms. Jo-Jo will calm down. Maybe I'll figure out how to watch my mouth. Maybe they'll change the name of the F.A.R.T. Maybe everybody will stop talking about cake. Maybe penguins will start giving each other foot massages. Maybe people will stop dropping bowling pins. Maybe Dr. Carbles will find a place to lay his eggs.

But it won't be easy!

More weird books from Dan Gutman

My Weird School

My Weird School Graphic Novels

My Weirder School

My Weirdest School

My Weirder-est School

My Weird School Fast Facts

My Weird School Daze

My Weird Tips